ISBN 0-439-63988-3

Text copyright © 1998 by Lori Haskins. Illustrations copyright © 1998 by Joe Mathieu. All rights reserved. Published by Scholastic Inc., 557 Broadway, New York, NY 10012, by arrangement with Random House Children's Books, a division of Random House, Inc. SCHOLASTIC and associated logos are trademarks and/or registered trademarks of Scholastic Inc.

12 11 10 9   9/0

Printed in the U.S.A.   40

First Scholastic printing, December 2003

TOO MANY DOGS

by Lori Haskins

illustrated by Joe Mathieu

SCHOLASTIC INC.

New York   Toronto   London   Auckland   Sydney
Mexico City   New Delhi   Hong Kong   Buenos Aires

Big dog.

Bigger dog.

Biggest dog of all.

Small dog.

Smaller dog.

Smallest of the small.

Waggy dog.

Shaggy dog.

Doggies in a bunch.

Floppy dog.

Sloppy dog.

Doggies eating lunch!

Sprinkly dog.

Wrinkly dog.

Scratchy dog.

Patchy dog.

Tricky dog.

Picky dog.

Happy, lappy, licky dog!

Spotty dog.

Dotty dog.

Doggies all about.

Howly dog.

Growly dog.

Doggies, please get OUT!

WOOF!